KU-178-420

The secret cave

William and Hamid were at the seaside. They
were staying in a cottage overlooking the beach.

'These cottages are hundreds of years old,' said
Hamid. 'They must have been here in the days of
pirates and smugglers. I bet it was exciting living in
those times.'

'Why don't we go and talk to old Captain Hood from
next door?' suggested William. 'I bet he used to
be a pirate. He looks like one.'

Captain Hood laughed when William asked him about
pirates and smugglers. 'Oh yes, boys,' he said.
'I could tell you stories that would make your hair
stand on end. Strange things happen at sea. Many times
I've had to tie myself to the wheel so that I wouldn't
be washed overboard by gigantic waves. And
the food was terrible. All we had to drink was
sea-water, and all we had to eat was ships' biscuits.
and any fish we could catch.'

2

'What did you use for bait?' asked Hamid.

'Worms from the ships' biscuits,' said Captain
Hood with a smile.

'But what about the pirates and smugglers?' asked Hamid. 'I've heard this village used to be famous for them.'

'It was indeed,' said Captain Hood. 'It was full of them.'

'But why?' asked William. 'Why should they want to come here?'

'It was all the caves, you see,' explained Captain Hood. 'The coast round here has hundreds of caves.'

'I see,' said William. 'That must have been where
they hid all their treasure.'

'You're right, my boy,' said the captain. 'I can
see you'd have made a good smuggler. On bright
moonlit nights the smugglers' ships used to drop
anchor in the bay out there. Then they would bring
their treasure ashore in rowing boats and hide it in
the caves.'

'What sort of things did they smuggle?' asked Hamid.

'Anything that people wanted,' smiled Captain Hood.
'Gold, tobacco, brandy, lemonade. You name it, they'd
smuggle it.'

William and Hamid decided to explore the caves.

'Do you think Captain Hood was telling the truth?' asked Hamid.

'I'm not sure,' said William. 'I've never heard of anyone smuggling lemonade before.'

There were lots of caves along the beach. Some of them were very small but some of them stretched a long way back into the darkness.

'We'd better be careful,' said Hamid. 'This could be dangerous.'

William and Hamid went into one of the big caves.

'I don't like it here,' said Hamid. 'It's spooky.'

'That's why it's a good place to hide treasure,' said William. 'I wonder if we'll find any?'

'Shouldn't think so,' said Hamid. 'People must have been looking for gold in these caves for years and years.'

William had been digging in the sand with his foot. Suddenly he let out a yell. 'Hamid! Come over here. I think I've found something.'

Hamid ran over to William and began to help him dig. 'What do you think it is?' he gasped.

'It feels like a wooden box,' replied William. 'And I think there are more of them.'

The boys scraped the sand away. There were several wooden boxes buried in the floor of the cave. They were so busy trying to dig out the boxes, that they did not notice a group of strangely dressed people watching them in the darkness.

'Oh, ho ho!' boomed a voice from the depths of the cave. 'What have we here?'

'Oh, no!' gasped Hamid. 'It's the smugglers!'

'What are you doing in my cave?' asked the leader. 'I'm Captain Irons, and these are my boxes. You wouldn't be thinking of stealing them would you?'

'Oh no,' said William. 'We're here on holiday. We were just having a stroll along the beach. We'd love to stay and talk to you about smuggling and pirates and things but I'm afraid we've got to go home for our tea now.'

One of the smugglers looked really fierce. He had tattoos on both his arms, a thick black beard, and a parrot on each shoulder.

'Don't trust them, Captain Irons,' he said. 'If we let them go they'll run and fetch the coastguards and we'll all be thrown in jail.'

'You're right, Blackbeard,' said the captain. 'Take them back to the ship. We'll need a couple of cabin boys on our next trip to Australia. We'll come back for the boxes when it's dark.'

The smugglers took William and Hamid to a big rowing boat that they had dragged on to the beach. A ship was anchored out in the bay.

'I'm afraid we really haven't got time to go to Australia,' said William. 'Mum will be expecting us home for tea.'

'Yes, and it's school on Monday,' said Hamid. The pirates just laughed.

'I think you're going to be late for school,' said Captain Irons.

'Yes, about four years late,' laughed Blackbeard. 'That's how long it takes to get to Australia and back.'

The pirates tied up William and Hamid and put them
in the hold of the ship. A pirate left them some
bread and cheese and a candle.

'Don't eat it all at once,' laughed Blackbeard.
'It's got to last you until we get to Australia.
We're going ashore for the boxes. They're full of
all the gold we've stolen.'

It was gloomy and damp in the hold of the ship. Hundreds of little eyes glinted in the candle-light.

'What are those?' asked Hamid.

'Mice,' said William, 'and they've given me an idea. If we rub the cheese on these ropes and then stay very still, the mice might chew through them.' William rubbed the cheese into the ropes on Hamid's wrists.

'All we can do now is wait,' said Hamid.

It took a long time but at last the mice chewed
through Hamid's ropes. He pulled himself free and
then untied William. The boys climbed the wooden
steps and crept out on to the deck of the ship.
Hamid didn't notice that he had kicked over the
candle that Blackbeard had left in the hold.

'There's nobody about,' whispered William.
'They've all gone ashore to get the gold.'

'Good,' said Hamid. 'I can see a little boat
tied up down there. Let's climb down the rope
ladder and row to the shore.'

It wasn't easy to row the little boat. Hamid
steered for the lights he could see in the cottages
above the beach.

When at last the boys landed, they were right alongside the smugglers' rowing boat. Hamid climbed into it. William heard him banging about in the darkness. 'What are you doing?' whispered William. 'You're making a terrible noise. They'll hear us if you're not careful.'

'I've made a hole in it,' said Hamid. 'Now they won't be able to escape back to their ship.'

Suddenly, there were lights near the mouth of the cave and the boys heard angry shouts from the smugglers.

'It sounds as if they're being chased by the coastguards,' said Hamid. 'We'd better hide behind that piece of driftwood.'

They were only just in time. The smugglers came running down the beach towards their boat. The coastguards came after them.

The smugglers tumbled into their boat and began to
row for their ship. Captain Irons and Blackbeard
escaped in the little boat that William and Hamid
had used.

The coastguards were too late to catch them
and stood on the beach shouting angrily and shaking
their fists.

'Yah! Boo! Can't catch us,' jeered the smugglers.

'Better luck next time!' laughed Captain Irons.
'You'll have to get up early in the morning to catch me!'

William and Hamid didn't move. 'We've escaped from
the smugglers,' whispered Hamid, 'but if the
coastguards see us they'll think we're part of
the gang.'

'Look,' whispered William. 'Look at that red glow
on the smugglers' ship. It's on fire.'

At that moment the smugglers in the rowing boat
began to shout. 'Help! We're sinking! Save us!'
Now it was the coastguards' turn to laugh and cheer.
The boat slowly disappeared under the waves and
the smugglers began to swim back to shore.

'Now we've got them!' shouted the coastguards.

The glow from the smugglers' ship grew brighter.
Captain Irons and Blackbeard still hadn't noticed it.
Instead of feeling sorry for their sinking friends
they fell about laughing. 'Goodbye, goodbye!'
laughed Captain Irons. 'Now there will be more
gold for us!'

Suddenly there was a terrific explosion. The smugglers' ship was blown into little pieces. A great wave flung Captain Irons and Blackbeard back on to the beach.

'Nice of you to drop in,' said the chief coastguard. 'Now you'll be clapped in irons, Captain Irons.'

William and Hamid heard a voice behind them.
'There's another two here,' said a coastguard.

'Yes,' said Blackbeard. 'They're our cabin boys
They are members of our gang too.'

'Run for it, Hamid!' shouted William. The boys
dashed towards the darkness of the cave and some
of the coastguards chased after them.

'Now we're trapped,' groaned William. 'How are we
going to get out of this mess?'

Hamid picked up a lantern that somebody had
left behind. 'There are some steps here,' he said.
'Come on! Let's see where they go.' The boys ran up
the steps. They could hear the coastguards close
behind them.

'There's a door,' shouted William. 'Quick, Hamid
it's our only chance!'

William and Hamid burst through the door and fell into the sitting room of their holiday cottage.

'What on earth are you doing hiding in that cupboard?' asked Mum. 'You're always hiding when I want you. Didn't you hear me calling you for tea?'

'But we were captured by smugglers,' said William. 'Then we had to escape from the coastguards. If we hadn't found the secret staircase we would have been in jail by now.'

'Oh William,' smiled Mum. 'What an imagination you've got. If it's not rats and mice and Pied Pipers, it's secret staircases in the broom cupboard.'

Hamid looked at William and shrugged. 'It's no good talking to grown-ups,' he sighed. 'They don't believe anything.'

After tea William and Hamid went next door to tell
Captain Hood about their adventure. Captain Hood
wasn't in but Mrs Hood was pleased to see them.
They told her what Captain Hood had said about the
smugglers, and about their adventure in the secret
cave.

'I think my husband has been telling you tall
stories,' laughed Mrs Hood. 'He's only been on a boat
once, and that was on the park lake. He even feels
sea-sick when he plays with his boats in the bath.'

'But why do they call him Captain Hood?' asked
William.

'Because he's Captain of the darts team, down
at the Smugglers Arms,' laughed Mrs Hood. 'That's
where he is now.'

Smugglers

At the Customs Office people have to pay a
tax on any expensive goods they may want to bring
into this country. A smuggler is somebody who tries
to bring goods into the country without paying taxes.

In the old days taxes on goods coming into the
country were high. Some of the fishermen who lived
round the coasts of Britain made a good living by
smuggling such things as brandy, wine, and tobacco.
A cask of brandy bought from a smuggler might cost
less than half the price of the same item bought from
a wines and spirits merchant.

Smuggled goods were landed from fishing boats at dead of night and hidden in caves, cellars, or even churches. Coastguards and Customs Officers tried to catch and punish smugglers but they had a hard time. Many ordinary people helped the smugglers trick the coastguards and were given a share of the smuggled goods.

In the old days sailing ships used to bring home rich cargoes of gold, ivory, and luxury goods from distant lands. There were people called pirates who thought it easier to steal goods from other ships than to go and fetch them themselves.

Pirate ships, full of fierce armed men, were feared by all traders. The pirate flag, the skull and crossbones, was enough to strike terror into the hearts of honest sailors.

The phantom ship

Ben had always wanted to go to sea so he signed up as a cabin boy on a ship called The Sea Lion. Captain Grimes was kind and friendly on shore but once at sea he grew fierce and ill-tempered. Ben began to wish he'd stayed at home. He had to work hard from dawn until late at night, and nothing he did pleased Captain Grimes.

One day as Ben was laying the table for the Captain's dinner, Grimes flew into a rage. 'Can't you get anything right?' he shouted. 'I'm expecting an important guest this evening. Get out the best silver. Nothing is too good for my visitor.' Ben wondered how anyone could visit a ship in the middle of the ocean but he didn't dare ask.

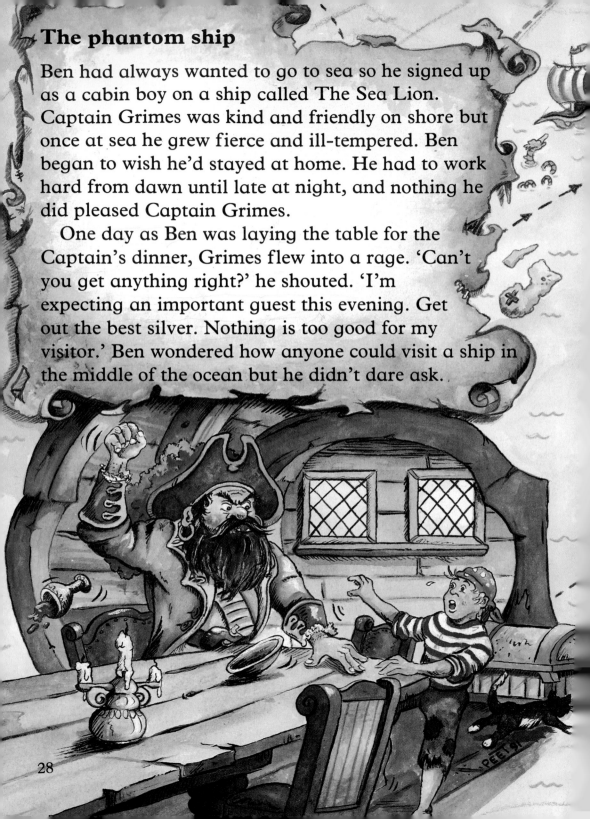

'Two for dinner tonight you say?' said the cook.
'Then I shall have to cook my best meal. The Captain
only uses the silver when he's expecting a visit
from the Dutchman.'

'Who is the Dutchman?' asked Ben.

'It's better that you don't know,' replied the cook.
When the meal was ready Ben carried the soup to the
Captain's cabin. He could hear Grimes talking
quietly and nervously. There was another voice
in the cabin. It sounded deep and harsh.

Ben tapped at the door and went in. There were
two places set at the table and two glasses of wine
but the Captain was sitting there alone.
Ben put the two bowls of soup on the table but as
he did so the ship gave a lurch and he spilled some on
the table-cloth.

With a furious shout Captain Grimes leapt from the table. 'You idiot!' he shouted. 'How dare you!'

'Leave the boy alone Grimes,' said the deep voice. 'Ever since you set sail you've been treating him badly. It must stop. Learn to treat your crew with respect or I shall leave you.'

Ben stared at the empty place from where the voice had come. His eyes grew wide as he saw a spoon float from the table and dip into the soup. He didn't wait to see anymore. He ran straight to the cook.

'There's nothing to be afraid of Ben,' explained the cook. 'The Dutchman is captain of the phantom ship. As long as he is with us, we'll have good luck. If we offend him we're sunk!'

'But I couldn't see him,' said Ben.

'Nobody has ever seen him,' said the cook.

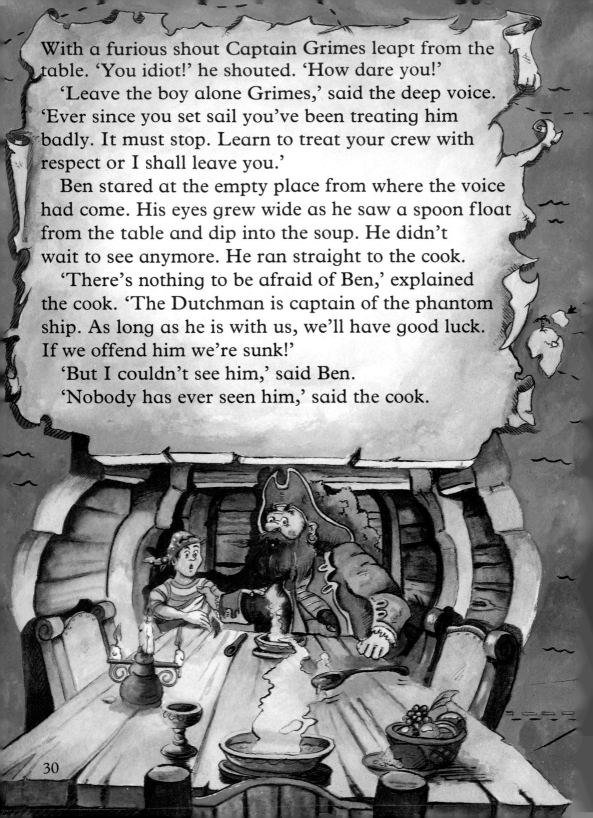

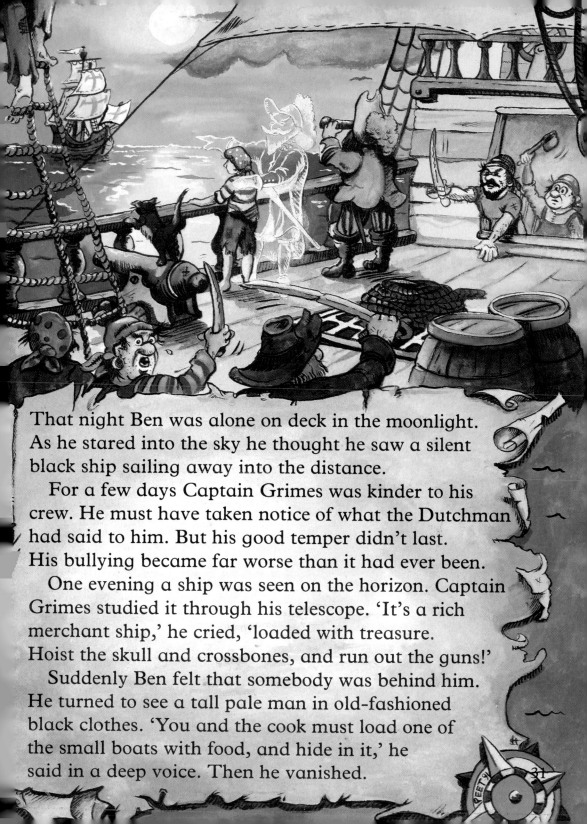

That night Ben was alone on deck in the moonlight.
As he stared into the sky he thought he saw a silent
black ship sailing away into the distance.

For a few days Captain Grimes was kinder to his
crew. He must have taken notice of what the Dutchman
had said to him. But his good temper didn't last.
His bullying became far worse than it had ever been.

One evening a ship was seen on the horizon. Captain
Grimes studied it through his telescope. 'It's a rich
merchant ship,' he cried, 'loaded with treasure.
Hoist the skull and crossbones, and run out the guns!'

Suddenly Ben felt that somebody was behind him.
He turned to see a tall pale man in old-fashioned
black clothes. 'You and the cook must load one of
the small boats with food, and hide in it,' he
said in a deep voice. Then he vanished.

The merchant ship was coming straight at The Sea Lion. Ben and the cook climbed into the little boat. With a deafening roar The Sea Lion's guns went off. But they didn't seem to do any damage. The merchant ship still came speeding towards them. As the two ships collided Ben saw the pale, dark stranger standing on the deck of the merchant ship.

'It's the phantom ship!' gasped the cook.
The Sea Lion sank to the bottom of the sea and the Dutchman sailed on into the night.

It was several days before Ben and the cook were rescued. The Captain of a passing ship welcomed them and treated them kindly. Ben never again saw the mysterious Dutchman nor the phantom ship. The legend says they must sail the seas forever. Who knows when and where they may next appear?